The

Passion

Play

JONATHAN LOVEJOY

Armageddon Publishing

Cover: *At the Edge of the Brook*, 1875
William Adolphe Bouguereau (1825-1905)

ISBN-10: 0692316566
ISBN-13: 978-0692316566

For every Mary

Green girl, green girl
Where have you been
I went around the world
And back again

Green girl, green girl
What did you see?
I saw the Devil
Looking at me

Green girl, green girl
What did you do?
I ran away—
And came back to you

Part One

That we henceforth be no more children, tossed to and fro, and carried about with every wind of doctrine, by the sleight of men, and cunning craftiness, whereby they lie in wait to deceive...

Ephesians 4:14

$\mathcal{S}$omeone had suggested, "Why can't Christ be a woman this time? God is a woman, right? Then it stands to reason that She redeemed the world through the blood of a woman…"

It was the kind of thing that shouldn't even have raised an eyelid. Turned a few stomachs, maybe, like when someone had painted the crucified Jesus upside down in a bottle of urine, or when they made that movie where he had sex with Mary Magdalene. But this was only a small time, small town art school play, that was so ridiculous the only uproar it should have caused was laughter.

Every so often it happens. An angry young artist will go into the story of Christ, and come out with his own interpretation. Reverential—never. But always about as scripturally accurate as Jesus Christ Superstar. My daughter's blasphemy had been inherent from the concept alone. The Christ was named after (Her) mother in the play, born of a virgin. The only difference being that God had manifested Herself as the baby Mary Jesus, and grew into the most beautiful little girl ever born, so lovely and demure that men had begged Joseph for her hand from the time she was twelve. But unlike other women, she had grown up acquainted with the scriptures, amazing even the rabbis at her intimate knowledge of the Law.

My daughter Caitlyn had claimed no allegiance to either side, frankly telling anyone who asked that she wrote the play out of pure frustration, not really caring if it got noticed or not, but knowing that it probably would. Anyway, she had decided she was going all the way with it, which she did, and she was floored when her school had actually agreed to stage it. They had called it *"...a scathing indictment on the paranoid, hypocritical religious culture, who have so little confidence in their own faith that they go ballistic whenever someone takes an artistic jab at it..."* The play will serve as an experiment, they said. If nothing else, to see what kind of reaction it will get from the community. A few eyebrows were raised early, when the lead actress was chosen. A young, large breasted ethnic beauty with smoldering eyes, brunette hair and golden light skin. All of her disciples, likewise, were women.

The university auditorium was filled to the rafters opening night, everybody knowing that at the very least, they were going to get a chance to see a sexy woman undergo the Passion, dragging the crucifixion wood across the stage until it was time to lay down upon it. Listening to her scream while they drove the pretend nails through her pretty yellow hands. If the production was good, she would be tied to the cross and lifted upright, where they could see Mary Jesus bare her blood covered breasts for the sins of the world.

They were not shocked when she did her Dance of the Last Supper, for her twelve disciples, disappointed that it had not degenerated into a multiple partner love fest. But her praying in the Garden of Gethsemane was interspersed with so much panting and writhing that the effect was unmistakably autoerotic. Topped off with a sincere, *"Heavenly Mother, if it be thy will, let this cup pass from me..."* followed by a scream for the ages, with the actress folding over to the floor of the stage beside the boulder. On cue, Andrea Judas sneaks in, flanked by the Roman soldiers clinking. The betrayal kiss proves climactic; a loving, nearly Romantic peck on the lips and a tight hug. The lady disciples scatter, while the soldiers grab their Lady Lord, dragging Her before the chief priests for trial.

"We know that all of your power comes from Satan himself. How else could a woman know so much about our Holy Scriptures? How else could you have performed these miracles, these blasphemies? Do you expect us to believe that you, a woman... can be the Messiah?"

The beautiful woman stands there on stage, head lowered, refusing to speak. One of the temple guards steps forward, and slaps her so hard that she grunts. Admonishing her to speak, which she does not.

Before long, she stands before the governor. The Lord and Savior Mary Jesus Christ is sent to be scourged. Bound to a stock facing the audience. Two soldiers haul back with more strength than is required, and without any sound effects, lay into the poor woman's back, full force. Her screams are obviously real, felt by everyone present. The bloody cat-o-nine tails had done the trick, causing one person in the audience to stand up and yell "Hey!" Someone quickly runs over to the poor man, and whispers that it is only special effects. Red dye. A crown of thorns is plaited—a bird's nest of sharp pointed needle-like protrusions—and is placed on the Lady Christ's head. The soldier hits the crown onto her head twice, eliciting a deep, bellowing, shaking cry from the Mary Jesus, complete with spit falling from her mouth. A dozen people have already gotten up to leave in horror, while the rest of the small auditorium has settled in for the ride.

We adore you
O Christ, and we praise you
Because by your Holy Cross
You have redeemed the world

They follow faithfully the beautiful, brunetted Daughter of Woman through every station, along the path of suffering. The stage actors endure boos and hisses, while staying the course of their mission, going through every part of the Passion Play. Those that know what hold their breath, waiting to see if a certain Station can be truly fulfilled. It is indeed, when the garment is torn from the bloody Mary Jesus, baring her incredibly large breasts to all who are present.

She is laid out upon the cross. Her arms are stretched and tied. Her hands are prepared for the nailing to the wood...

Then suddenly, loud thunder sounds through the auditorium. Every stage actor stands frozen in motion. The word *"sin"* is hissed serpentine through the speakers (electronically altered), the voice of the young actress recorded. The stage lights are dimmed, and a spotlight shines on the Mary Jesus, who writhes in place on her horizontal cross, repeating the word sin over and over, in an increasingly evil, raspy voice. She breaks her bonds, turns over onto the stage floor, and begins to crawl in a slinky, snakelike fashion, breasts hanging exposed, calling the disciple Mary Magdalene to life.

Mary Magdalene leaves the side of the Lady Christ's mother, and goes over to where Mary Jesus is standing, away from the cross. She hisses *"let me see it... let me see your [backside],"* the word *backside* being a vulgarity clearly spoken, saying it all very angrily, with force and passion. Mary Magdalene obliges, now in the spotlight with the heroine, with her robe raised, exposing herself to the Lady Messiah from the rear. The Mary Jesus begins to slap her bare buttocks repeatedly, hissing demonically, *"I will have your sin... give your sin to me..."* She gets to her knees, crawling, snaking into position, and the disciple Mary Magdalene kneels behind her, and thrusts against the Mary Jesus repeatedly while she screams to the rafters of the theater like a monster.

Mary Magdalene returns to her place on the darkened stage beside mother Mary. Then, the Lady Christ stands still, blood stained breasts still exposed, looking toward heaven devoutly. She walks slowly back to the horizontal cross. She lays down upon it, and the stage lights go up again, while every actor begins to move. The soldiers secure her arms and legs to the beam with tight leather straps.

And when the soldiers nail, the Lady Christ screams to the rafters, entranced now by her calling, sending chills through every spine. They nail her hands to the cross, immersed in a new wave of shrieks and screaming.

The cross is lifted impressively upright, and the Mary Jesus is crucified for the sins of the world.

> *Holy Mother! Pierce me through*
> *In my heart each wound renew*
> *Of my Savior crucified*

When the article appears in the local newspaper the very next day, "Campus Play Causes Controversy," My daughter actually says, "Yes!" to herself out loud, knowing that every young playwright should be so lucky. She is particularly struck by the article's satisfyingly vicious closing line... *"one person who saw the play called it 'the most vile, disgusting, tasteless piece of filth they had ever seen.'"*

Caitlyn Sweet kisses the article. Laughing out loud. Secure in the knowledge that her future is set. When she gets to her dorm room, the stares and whispers hardly seem to bother her as she makes her way to the elevator. After all, she is the author. Who knows, *The Passion Play* could appear off Broadway someday. Who cares if they are jealous, right?

The elevator door opens to the ninth floor, revealing a soft chattering of girls, who are not really girls at all, but young women. One of them passes by her, getting into the elevator, saying, *I'm sorry about what happened.*

Bewilderedly, Caitlyn watches the elevator door close. She begins to walk toward her dorm room, watching the girls (many of whom she despises) begin to disperse. She feels herself walking slower, until it seems as though she is floating above the uncarpeted hall. From her vision, her mind suddenly registers blood red, in lines and markings across her white door. As she approaches, the lines click in her brain, merging together into letters and words, spray painted in dripping red paint across her white dorm room door—

"Thou shalt not suffer a witch to live…"

*E*mily was in the 9th grade when Caitlyn was killed.

Since the day I saw Caitlyn's blood blasted out of her back through her pink sweater, her sister's heart began to keep rhythm in my ears. The music of the beating heart. The ticking of a clock. In the 8 years since she died, I wonder if I have allowed her 8 seconds in my mind. Even so, like a cold breeze in autumn, she still tries to visit me.

I'm lucky enough to be living a dream. Even if it is without my daughters. My husband was generous enough to divorce me and marry another woman. Without knowing it, he answered a prayer I had always prayed, though I hadn't known it at the time. So how can I blame him then, for leaving me after my daughter was killed? Something in me drove him away, I'm sure.

I am Forgotten. Somewhere in modern history. And though time is irrelevant, I have marked it by my other daughter's footsteps. Through her 9th grade year, even to the summer of her graduation from high school.

The train only kills the ones who never see it coming. When their eyes are too glassed over with joy, and their ears are stuffed with cotton laughter. We had one of the most beautiful houses in Charlotte. The light colored bricks. The tall white pillars were not stained with her blood. Only the big white door. That was eight years ago. Eight minutes. Eight seconds ago, the Charlotte breeze on Megan-Elizabeth Drive kisses the invisible remains. A world, and a lifetime away, I am cursed to live a dream anew. Miles, and many lands east, beyond where Megan-Elizabeth blackness lays. Here I rest. Astroll these fields of green grass down east, where I call homeland. Down east, on the far outskirts of Williamston. Tobacco country, where Sir Raleigh's name is supreme. Where the Bible Belt is King.

The worthy elite, were we. Caitlyn, Emily, and Mary Sweet were three. How much is Predestiny? How much of it is ourselves? The curses that plague the lives we live? This is the one that put my husband into the ground after he left me, less than a month into his new marriage. Fate left his will in such generous tone. Which sang a melody to me, *leave Charlotte!* Take thy daughter and run! I found my dream on 52 acres of barren farmland. Unwanted. With a six room shanty. A house, if I'm thankful. For as far as the eye can see, there is only space, with pine trees afar off. To remind me that perhaps a world lies beyond my own, even beyond the setting sun, which I try to bid farewell to nightly.

I am not a country girl. Nor a farm woman. I am only fear, and dread of each coming night, and the sound of voices not my own. And though I try to tell myself I am not afraid of people, though I act as brave as the pioneer, I know in my heart that I have left society behind forever. Emily was resigned to this when she left me four years ago, to go to the University. This same campus in Greensboro, where the Passion Play was given. So far west of here. Though why she would go, I can never know. What is the harm of staying here among the flowers in our yard, the leaves of the grassy field beyond, to rest alone here with me? I told her that we could be content together for all time. I had her dead father's guilt money, and social security for my sickness. What needs do we have, except for a cloudless sky at sunset, and when the stars come out at night?

But in the spirit of youth, she leaves me to disability. Unguilty. She, for leaving. Me, for staying. These acres are my salvation. Here, miles and worlds away, I am not haunted by Caitlyn's grave.

My Emily's grave, I tend.

$\mathcal{P}$aula Abdul. Though I am not sure why. Her teeth. Her smile and her body are just perfect. I am a mother. Not gay or bisexual. But she's only one of the women I have fantasized about. It is the nature of women. Selective Bisexuality is the nature of women. Men do not have this, outside of perversion. Male homosexuality is a clear perversion. Lesbianism is clearly a *di*version. Frowned upon as perverse, though it is normal. Some women even fantasize about their daughters, although I never did. Did I imagine the severest punishments, however? With them naked over my knee? When the storm of Caitlyn began, this I did imagine—so that she would come to her senses. She never did.

The last year of her life begins in earnest. Even I am excited. I know she has been writing all summer. She says it is the play to end all plays. Neither of us can hear what she is saying. The words register their clownish tone, to hide their true meaning. I draw more importance and depth from the opening of her tuition envelope. With some of her father's guilt money, this I gladly pay. The first bill of her last year as an undergraduate. In ignorance, I pay. It is like buying a ticket for the death train. I coalesce, until I am able to see her. A beautiful face, which she hides in no makeup and behind glasses. Her hair is golden sunlight, as is my own. Her curves are apparent in the tight shirts and jeans. Modern women are eaten alive by exhibitionism. The need to show their hips and breasts through form fitting clothes. Caitlyn Sweet is no exception. Neither is her mother, or her 14 year old sister. When Caitlyn is 22, she will die.

Explosions rattle the far corners of my mind. In the night, there are fools rattling the cages of their fate. Satan's light is upon them. Even at 14, Emily's face and body are beyond reason. How is it that nature gives so much to some? Her hair is brown. Her eyes are blue. Already, her breasts are heavy, like my own. Beauty is her calling card, even at 14, though her personality is as her last name. She is Divine. In her smile is nothing of her older sister's mindless, incessant drive and chatter. She is worthy of her name. When she is 18, she will die on the highway at night. Her blood will mix with the broken glass, twisted metal, and the white airbag that will deploy stupidly. A curse. Swift and long. Born of sin. Shapen in iniquity.

Why wasn't I told? Why did they let me believe that the dream was prosperity? When I saw my dream daughter in the black limosine pull up to the house, I was not afraid. When I saw her get out of the car, dressed entirely in black, the spirits showed me no raven. There was only peace, that Caitlyn was assured a future of joy and prosperity. Her black dress and hat are of a design unknown. Beauty incarnate. Taste and modesty. Her blonde hair and perfect face are in such glowing contrast to the dress and hat that it is painful to see. She is the picture of health and beauty. In the rain, in the gentle mist, she glides the fine brick walkway towards our house. The white columns tower in my mind. What are you doing here, Daughter? Aren't you supposed to be in school? I do not see Death in the black. I see Life. Joy, riches and fame. I see the lust of the eyes. The pride of life. Caitlyn, my sweet, I see the glory of the Lord in your eyes.

When I awake from this dream, I am happy.

*W*hen I think of Caitlyn, I grow angry. Am I angry with her for dying, or with myself for letting her die? I think I bear responsibility, because I did not teach her the Truth. Somewhere in my heart, I say, how could she believe such an unnatural lie? While I sit and listen to her tell me that it's possible that Jesus was a woman, I think I laugh for the same reason I laugh at the Christ-Magdalene theory. But I would not laugh, if I could see that Death bears no joy when it touches. The Death of others, whom we do not love, can evoke a giggle. But when those we love have died, it is the lowering of outer darkness into our lives. Here, there is weeping and gnashing of teeth.

I should have had the common sense, the basic moral instinct, to tell her no. Jesus was not a woman. The same as not being Mary Magdalene's husband, he was not a woman. Neither did He any sin. My daughter's pseudo-intellectual power, confidence from three years of reading and writing foolishness and nonsense; she tells me of some person, some thing that inhabits space as a human being named Ellen Sopper*stein*, who convinced her that Jesus may have actually been a *woman*. That there is a lost gospel, *The Gospel of Elizabeth*, on which the four gospels are based. That *She* sent *her* only begotten daughter. That the Mother God inspired the Holy scriptures from Genesis to Revelation. That this was buried without controversy by the early church, because no sane man or woman would want to be identified with Mary *Elizabeth*; Mary Jesus Christ, and would have never worshipped her as the Messiah. I know now that this kind of doctrine is sickness, the deepest perversion, perhaps a greater blasphemy than even to deny God's existence. Of this, I cannot pretend to be ignorant. Ellen Sopper*stein* breathed a curse into my daughter's mind, where it grew. It infected her blood and was carried into every muscle and bone, into every nerve fiber and to every cell of her body. This grew to disease proportions, until she became sick with it. It contaminated her lungs, where she coughed and breathed it into the air, endangering every person she spoke to thereafter. But even though she is still away, in her junior year East when she hears the blasphemy, the curse already flows laterally, through the branches of the river, the streams of her family's tree.

This curse, breathed into the air by Satan, to mock the name of our Lord, to make fun of those who could only turn their noses upwind of this stench, and could never entertain even the possibility of the hypothetical. Even the atheist, the murderer, the brawler, the rapist, the kidnapper, the child abuser, the wife and husband beater, the liar, the thief, the adulterer, the idolator. Even all of these and some I cannot mention, know where to draw the line. The line is in the heart, where it is crossed by some, where their first step beyond is a permanent problem, indeed. For me, for my soon to be ex-husband and his wife, for my dearest Emily Anne, this has crept up to where we live and breathe, until the smoke tickles our throats with ashe and disease. The curse of sin. When she first speaks to me of it, I laugh. Giggling as much about the idea of Jesus being God, as him being a woman.

Ellen Sopper*stein*. Ellen Sopper. A feminist, though she could never admit it. She is the source of my daughter's incurable disease. The sickness that will take her life. But how is it, that this same Ellen, believing that the Mary Jesus died on the cross for her sins, could also subscribe to so many old anti-Christ theories, that apply to the man Christ-Jesus? What contradiction is it, that she and so many atheists fight the God they claim they don't believe in? The "Swoon Theory", that Christ really *was* resurrected, because he didn't die, but fainted *near* death due to trauma and loss of blood. The "Theft Theory," that the disciples stole his body. The "Body Removal Theory," that the Romans or the Jewish authorities took him. The "Wrong Tomb" theory, that Mary Magdalene was at the wrong burial site that morning. The "Nostalgia Theory," that Christ's resurrection occurred only in the hearts of his disciples. The "Imposter Theory," that someone took Christ's place on the cross. The "Hallucination Theory," that

Christ's resurrection was a figment of the disciple's imagination, and so on infinitum.

The things that Caitlyn spoke to me that summer. That summer before her senior year. *I know it's stupid, Mom. I know it's ridiculous, Mom. No, I don't believe it, it's just an interesting theory, Mom.* Why then, are you going to blaspheme their Holy Play? Why, then, are you going to blaspheme *The Passion*?

God is not a woman.

But She gave birth to the universe. She has to be a woman. Matthew 23:37 says *"O Jerusalem, Jerusalem, thou that killest the prophets, and stonest them which are sent unto thee, how often would I have gathered thy children together, even as a hen gathereth <u>her</u> chickens under <u>her</u> wings, and ye would not."* God's *wisdom* is a *<u>female</u>* in Proverbs 1:20, and 9:1— and Jesus is called the *<u>wisdom</u>* of God in 1 Corinthians 1:24. Her real name was Mary *Elizabeth*, and Elizabeth means *The Promise of God*. She couldn't have had a daughter with Mary Magdalene because they were both women, Caitlyn says.

It does not click in my mind. Why should it? When someone speaks of a disaster on the football field, what woman can truly sympathize? Caitlyn is a football coach to me at this moment, screaming at me of some silly calamity, which is only a game I care nothing about. She is a cook yelling at me in Italian, and I am over a bowl of flour in tears, holding eggs. I do not know from whence she speaks, this daughter of mine, unreligious in her tank top and big-C cleavage. Reading a feminist religious article. Alas I am safe! She will turn her English Literature / Theater major into a pot of gold weave, spun through the wheel of teaching! She will forget this stupidity of Christ being a woman, and return to her senses.

But what is it to me? I know nothing of Christ, whether She be God or no. This August, just beyond the Century, four years before the death of melody! Her melody will be 18, when it ceases its voice to sing! A curse, brought to us by Caitlyn Sweet, upon thy demonic muse's wing! *I need your sin,* the Lady Christ will say—*Give your sin to me!*

$\mathcal{T}$he heat of the August night blows dust over the Desert Moon. I am at peace on Megan Elizabeth Drive—arms folded, eyes half closed, gazing our suburban paradise. My two daughters are in my palace. My angel columns tower above me, to protect me from the Spirit of Poverty. But down the street I see the shadow of premonition, stalking towards the house. The shadows carry their shadowy weapons, long and sleek. To blast a hole in—no. It is only the neighbor's jock son, and the silly hockey sticks he carries as though he lived beside a frozen pond in northern Canada. He is a southern wannabe fool, too stupid to know that his youth is being drained, that his strength is drying up through misdirected energy. When he is 22, he will be a burned out shell, ready to be filled with the corporate philosophy. Having peaked this very summer of his 18th year on this Earth.

Why does the Charlotte breeze, the warm hazy twilight wind, blow me such a cold kiss? Why does it take form upon my walkway to say, *Hey witch!* The sound of a firecracker and a scream shake me to the bone. My blood runs cold under the Desert Moon. Big and orange in the evening. Caitlyn is hard at work upstairs. I think I can hear her scratching the words onto the paper. Her writer's gift, manifested when she was nine, is awakened. God is a woman tonight. I shrug my shoulders. What do I care if He is a She? It makes more sense anyway. Does it not?

Emily is coming. I can feel her spirit aflight down our palatial stairs. Her hand touches the doorknob. She comes outside to me.

Yes, Caitlyn *is* crazy.

She won't let me in her room and I need to get my phone back from her.

You can use mine—

My sweet.

What candy tastes as sweet, as a kiss from the lips of an Emily? Her lips are pink, and too big for her beautiful little face. They are soft against mine. Even now, we are not afraid of the full hug, which sees our bosoms together in the moonight. Emily and I are one. We are not afraid to press our lips in the long moan, something less than a kiss, more than a simple touching. We are not afraid, Emily and me. Above us, on the eve of cataclysm, I hear the scratching. The etchings on their tombstones. Scratching themselves to life.

She is her father's daughter. He rolls home in luxury unnamed, pewter gray. Piercing blue eyes and deadly chiseled features. Smiling at his trophy wife and daughter. His receding hairline makes him look like a handsome clown. He is filled with the pride of accomplishment. His voice is laced with arrogance, disguised in perpetual good humor. His pockets bulge with money. His corporate heart is black with printer's ink. He stinks of old cologne as he kisses my daughter. His youngest daughter. Now, in front of her, I must whore my lips to his crusted mouth, lips chapped from eight hours of office breathing and walking and running and sitting and $189,000 dollars a year for doing absolutely nothing. He feels nothing of my resentment. The ice of it remains in my heart, formed anew. As he walks away, the heat of my daughter's affection melts it away, even though she follows him into the house, to beg of some tasty dinner treat. I call after her helplessly. Happy. Unhappy. Content. Unsettled.

I see a land far away from here! Where there are no houses and trees to burden my eyesight, except for the trees of the prairie green. I desire to be free!

Why does this woman walk her dogs with such angry energy? Where is she going? Is she going to walk her hips away? Tomorrow they will be as big and misshapen as they are tonight. The dogs are her children, moreso than her spoiled rotten son and daughter. Why does the other woman jog with such energy? Huffing and puffing to impress. Yes, your blonde ponytail bobs up and down beautifully. Yes, your young body is tight and perfect, though I prefer my own curviness to yours. It is softer. More feminine to the eye. My body pleases me, so that I may eat and relax, to keep my curves where they be. Whose husband do you require? Certainly not your own!

I wave at my nosy neighbor. Though I secretly cannot stand the sight of her. I loathe, I despise every inch of her short black hair and her fat smiling face that everyone speaks of with such fondness. You are a nosy phony! Get thee back to thine own abode!

While every car cruises into their spaces. While every one of them goes inside those grand $700,000 homes, I know what churns beneath cultured civility. It is the same that had bled into my future, to take my daughters away from me. I listen as the almighty hypocrite, on my visits to their houses, on their visits to mine, and I know of the children arrested for drug possession, the abortions done in secret, the cocaine sniffed in private, the prescription highs and lows, the domestic violence, the alcoholism, the affairs, the child abuse, the male adultery with other men, the female adultery with other women. I know what churns beneath cultured civility; of how at least one of the neighborhood daughters is disciplined with a nude hairbrush spanking by her mother, and that the burn on another's back is not from leaning against a hot metal lamp post. They smile in the light, though in the darkness they grimace in the pain of their lives. I stand on my fine lawn. Judging them, as if I am superior. Am I superior to them? I am not.

What churns beneath cultured civility?

I hate my husband.

What churns beneath cultured civility?

I am afraid of my oldest daughter.

What churns beneath cultured civility?

I worship my youngest daughter.

$\mathcal{E}$mily's begging to her father has prevailed. It is time for our last meal together as a family. Will it be steak, chicken, ribs, Chinese, or seafood? Pizza. Caitlyn is distant as we go. Her mind is occupied. She tells her father nothing of her new project—how she is going to assure herself of greatness even before graduation. We marvel at the Desert Moon as we drive. The last full moon before Labor Day. Before summer ends as it is measured by the heart, though it is still summer long after, by the ticking of the clock. We cruise the wealthen stream, a pretty quartet. One in pride—another in arrogance—one in naivite—another in misery. I am neither proud, arrogant nor naïve.

In million dollar contentment, we stuff ourselves. Elite. Glad that we are not like so many of them. We are whitewashed. Clean. Spotless. Unblameable. We are perfect, the four of us. On the surface, we are happy. How far have you gotten in your play, I ask. She shrugs off the question, and I know not to ask again. I am afraid to ask again. But I notice that even the thought of it raises tension in the air, like a frozen echo from the future. Gerald asks, what play? I try to spill the words, needing to badly. But in her bold, thin, hippy, big chested way, my scholarly doll—my salty doll—says nothing, just a dumb play I'm working on. It's not finished, so I can't talk about it. She gazes me a look of fury, burning blue and black fire. These are the fires of rage and violence, both sometimes done quietly, where the burning is slow.

The teenage waitress works hard to hide her low self esteem. Her face is puffy and rounded, as is her body. My daughters freeze her cold in fear. Her look at them is fearful. In my heart, I am sorry for her mother.

A truck pulls into the parking space outside the window. It reminds me of guns and ammunition. The man and woman inside are white like us, but they are more comfortable being loud. I can see it in their body language. The woman is pretty enough to cause me to squirm in my chair. I bless the almighty God that Gerald, Caitlyn and Emily did not see her. The truck, I think they saw. They are white trash to me. I am jealous of their freedom. I despise their affection for one another. The love that they have for their fellow man makes me sick to my stomach. My charity is superior. I am called to make the world a better place, am I not? How dare they pretend to be so happy? So free. I am better than they are. My husband is better looking. I am more beautiful than she. I am richer. It would take them eight years to earn our income for one year.

Caitlyn. Emily! Husband! I am sick at heart! My breasts are heavy with premonition! The way we are is sickening to me! My superior self is a clamour in my ears! Our talk of money and school and graduate school and careers is Death to my appetite. Heavenly Father, I beseech thee! I beseech thy throne! Have mercy for me!

My husband is having an affair. She is a lollipop with a big pretty head. My breasts and bottom are his boredom after twenty four years. Had he married her first, her lovely bones would be his boredom. She will bury his, a month after they are married. The tall brunette salivates at the thought of being Mrs. Dale Fitzgerald Sweet. Her name is Shannon. The idea of her real estate business cards makes her heart race. Who would not buy an upscale home from such a name? She will bide her lovely time, through this long year, through our coming divorce and tragedy, then into their brief tomorrow. I was married when she was born. She will want children. She will never conceive without trouble. She will never carry a child to term. Her marriage after Gerald's death will be unhappy, with the severest emotional neglect. He will call her a skinny birdface, which will reduce her to tears in private, as she thinks her thinness is pleasing even to the Gods. But now, she is cozy in lithe posture. Her wispy, graceful stride, her long legs. Her statuesque, effervescent flow, as the white winged sylphide, or even as the lilies of the Messiah field.

I am not a prisoner of time and space. Only grief. I go where I will, where I want, to see who and what I need to see. To rid my soul of this poison.

Two weeks away from our quiet dinner, Emily and I are at the threshold of a new life. A journey, beginning inside Caitlyn's campus dorm room. The building is white, to resemble the ivory tower that it is. She is so focused and independent, so happy to be here that my mind is at ease when we hug. It is a strange hug, one where I hold on for too long, squeezing too tight. Mom I'm not dying, she says. I know. I'm just going to miss you so much this year. Next time we see you will be Thanksgiving. It's just three months. I take off her ridiculous black rimmed lawyer nerd focals so I can see her eyes. Behind the glasses and the unadorned face are features extraordinary to look at. But I know that beauty is not her game. Talent. Intellect. Insight. Wisdom. These are the lights that sparkle in her eyes.

She gives her younger sister a big hug. I study the hug, to see what song it will sing. It plays a melody of longing, colored by harmonies of regret. Longing from the younger, who does not know her twenty one year old sister who is so smart, so full of unadorned prettiness and wit, who is an independent soul. A free spirit at heart. There is regret from the older, that she does not know her 14 year old sister, being away from home since long before her womanhood began to show. They are connected through the bloodline, though not in the spirit, for it is through the ancestry that all recompense curses flow.

Caitlyn does not escort us through the long hall to the elevator. The empty hall where our footsteps have come to know. The echo of our footsteps are now among where these spirits flow. These are spirits of unworthy ambition—unholy strivings to see paradise on earth—that created by money, prestige and power. This is Melancholy Hall, where Emily and I are adrift.

As my luck would have it, these summer skies are ashen gray, as if they tell of future rain and worry. We walk unashamedly out of place, the shapely two of us in our T-shirts and jeans. The forty something and the teen, the 14 year old version of the same. We find our way to silver gray luxury, and know that the first drop of rain is held from us until we get inside. Of the black cat that was curled cozily in the rear of our car, we see it walking a distance away now. We back out of the space, and our world is shaken to its foundations by a thunderous metallic crash, a muffled crunk, and our car is moved nearly diagonal from where it sat.

A student. Racing carelessly through the parking lot, slamming into us. Oh, Holy Day! Oh Blessed Night! We will set our credit card and cell phone in motion! To have our wreckage towed to a body shop, then to rent some other beauty on wheels. My first call is to my angel brain in the dorm, to tell her the exciting news. We are not coming up, however. We will rent our car, and hurry back to Charlotte before the gray begins to rain.

The tow truck driver is kind. He seems happy to help the busty white older woman and her buxom little beauty. It's not too bad, he says. A couple thousand, I think. He says this because we reek of money. He mentions Greg's Auto Repair, but I kindly defer to him to talk of Maaco. His memory is faulty, but he knows where it is. Our ride in his grungy cab is unmercifully long. He talks incessantly about his wife. I'm glad. It eases the tension. Something about his wife and physical therapy. I cannot care. When we arrive, he is kind enough to offer further assistance. Do I ride with him, or take a cab to the car rental place? A cab will do. I lie to him, telling him that I may need it to take me to the bank first for more cash. My card is at its limit, I say. Does the poor man believe my lie? He does. Thankfully, the big tow truck pulls away. Inside the Maaco, I locate the number for a taxi. While I call, I am glad that I will never see that man again.

The cab takes nearly a half hour to arrive. An excruciating wait. Something about the rain, and more calls. And sorry, Maam. Pain has a face. It is a bearded man with old, wrinkled eyes. A nice cab, it is. A

Dodge Intrepid. Midnight Blue. Pain drives us to a car rental lot. It is not Avis or Heartz. I don't see a single car I would like to rent here. They all look used. Emily picks out the white Ford Thunderbird, which I don't mind. We will have to come back in four days to retrieve our silver gray luxury.

Black cat conundrums and cookie drums. Mums the word for me.

Black cats really are bad luck, huh Mom?

Where's the bad luck, I ask. She is afraid to answer. We didn't get hurt and our car will be fixed by Friday. And we're on our way home in this nice car, right?

Yeah.

They are mending your chariot, my dearest Emily. Your chariot to eternity.

My heart echoes the Dance of the Swans—the winds are as light as a feather. They are colored azure, while the basses are heavy cloud mountains of snowy white. It is the song of my little girl's demise, as we glide the streets west, from where the origin of these curses lie. Why was I physically unnerved by the pretty black cat, which did not run away from Emily? I told her no, don't touch it. You don't know where it's been or who it belongs to. She gently shooed it away with her shoe. I did not watch it walk away while I undid the lock, though in my heart I did dread the color of the confounded yellow-eyed beast. I know it is stygian, from the forest along the shores of Hades. Those who see the Stygian are the most unfortunate among women. I struggle to bear the sounds of youth from these unfamiliar speakers, which seem not as powerful as our own, though no less noisy.

They are mending your chariot, my dearest Emily. Your chariot to eternity.

I see Caitlyn ignoring her books and her clothes. Her mind is on fire again. Given muse from the academic surroundings; colored by the spirits of the dead, the cemetery that is academic life. It is death to the soul. While she lays down this new law, as she digs the foundations for her tower, I see diggings of another kind, and my heart aches for her to abandon the sacred ground, before it is too late. But she scribbles away her life with pencil. No pen. No word processor. Just the paper before half closed eyes, obeying nothing of the lines, to allow the passion to break free from her mind.

Along the valleys and hills of Palestine. Among the groves of trees and vines, past the plains of golden wheat and barley grain, she strolls the streets of the City of David, to see the Virgin Mary, with the baby girl in her arms. The baby whimpers only when it needs to be fed. The child's eyes are clear and blue, though her hair will be as black as the night sky over Bethlehem. Her beauty, her chastity, are to greatly distinguish her from every woman ever born, as will her knowledge of the Holy Scriptures, and the ways of the Almighty God.

She watches the child grow in stature, in dignity and poise unheard of for such a young girl. She is her father's child in spirit, though she takes up the chores and duties of her calling. The girl sees her father's profession, to often intervene with instinct, to display inherent skill of the carpenter's hand. In all of Nazareth, there is no child likened to her, with such grace and beauty, and devotion unheard of for the ways of the Lord our God. Even at 12, the men look upon her with broken hearts, with spirits tormented, knowing that while they ask for her hand, some offering a king's dowry, God hath already refused their prayer. And none but her mother and father know the secret, that this child, whom they call Mary *Elizabeth,* bears the hidden name Yeshua, which means "Salvation."

Mary, Daughter of Joseph. Who increases in wisdom and loveliness. Taller than every other woman they have seen, to possess eyes of such power as to cause fear, though not of desire, but humility unrestrained. Speaking with such spiritual authority as to evoke a sense of weeping. Those who hear her look to every other woman with reverance in their heart, and worship of the Lord. They long not for her beauty in their heart, and are not taken by her eyelids, but they return from her face to their closet of prayer, to ask forgiveness for every improper inkling of the soul. They look upon this woman, and dare not ask whenceforth she came, nor to where it is she may go. All near and abroad speak of Mary of Nazareth, the Daughter of Joseph, and of the manner in which she may live and speak. The playwrite feels the gaze of this Mary's blue eyes, eyes of an angel. Her black hair fallen about her shoulders and the length of her back, though often covered by cloth, so that only the beauty of her face is shown.

Her height is such that most men must see her eyes at their level, or even to gaze up at her. She is taller than her cousin the Baptist at the river Jordan, who proclaims the coming of the Lamb of God, who taketh away the sins of the world. The prophetess preaches with fire, to burn conviction through all who hear, that apart from those who dismiss her as insane, there are some who believe, and wait for the coming of the Lady Messiah. The Lady Baptist proclaims her arrival, from the Star of Bethlehem and the journey of the Magi, and their gathering to the stables with treasures for the child in the manger. Joseph speaks her chosen name, while his wife speaks the name given to her by God. The child's mother speaks her name to them, and they weep.

From the child, to the woman at the River Jordan. The Baptist dips her hands in the cool of the waters, and baptizes all who come to be cleansed. But she dips her hands the last time, and looks up to see the eyes of who she has seen only in her dreams, this being the Chosen One. The blood of the Lady Baptist runs cold with revelation and fear, knowing it is her who needs baptism from She. But they commence the Holy Baptism, so that the scriptures are fulfilled. All who are present hear a voice, as the sound of thunder, proclaiming this is my Beloved daughter, in whom I am well pleased. She walks away from the river, being filled with the Holy Spirit, in the power of God, into the wilderness to fast and pray, and be tempted by the Devil.

I get the call near the end of October, underneath the Harvest Moon. The leaves cloak themselves in Autumn colors, to protect them from the chill of their deaths. On the phone, Caitlyn is shrieking in my ear of something, I do not know what. Something about passions and plays, Ellen Sopperstein and the UNCG Theater. I'm a playwrite, she yells. But how can I be glad for her. *I'm going to be executed,* might as well be her celebration. It would bring me just as much joy as this does. None. What it brings is the chill of Autumn, and a breath of the coming winter. While I congratulate her on this success, this arrival of the Queen of the Jews, my mind races to the very day's events, and to my daughter's bloody nose. Not blood from sicknesss or a bumping against the door, but from a fight at school. My daughter. My Sweet Anne, who goeth gently upon the days. My Emily was in a fight. Though one she claims she did not start. Every teacher, every student, me and my husband, all blown away by even the idea of her being violent.

She is upstairs. Resting with her music on the phone, suffering a terrible bump on the head. There is a girl at her new school, high school, where every kind and class of student attends. There is a girl of the lower classes who lives in a trailer, so I hear. So I know. So I see. Her name, by God, is Fancy. Fancy hears that Emily called her a slut behind her back. And she also hears that a boy she likes likes Emily instead. My Sweet Emily, oh how I pray she does not care for it all! This girl finally, after weeks of rumors, lies and threats, approaches Emily and tells her, if you don't fight I'm going to *beat your ass you punk bitch*—what words are these! They did find their way into the world, to my daughter's virgin ears! In the locker hall, this very morning before school! This Fancy Comfort let my daughter's hair, her perfect Doll's eyes and skin, her hourglass shaped young body, turn her sanity until there was nothing left for her to give but rage and retaliation. My daughter is the unattainable to her, the symbol of her own unfulfilled desire, the reason for her failure thus far. Emily embodies everything she cannot have, every privilege she will never know. My daughter is the barrier between her and freedom, between her and life itself.

She corners Emily, against the wall of eyes that stare. There, in the lunchtime cafeteria, Fancy Comfort approaches Emily Sweet, and tells her to get up from the table. My Emily tucks her lips at first, so terribly afraid. But in the peer pressure, under the weight of staring, her teenage sensibility shatters to pieces, and she lets her station in life rise up, and spew a superior, self assured laugh. The bigger, heavier, stronger Fancy grabs my daughter by her black jenny-braids, claiming *I heard what you've been saying behind my back*. My daughter looks at her. So pretty. So beautiful. So content. So complacent. She touches her braid in place again, down the front of her snow white sweatshirt, and shakes her head. While Fancy stands there, humiliated, a laugh cannonballs from somewhere in the cafeteria and smashes her resolve to rubble.

She grabs my daughter's hair, pulls her from the table and throws her to the floor, making her bump her head. Emily cannot cover her face in time to prevent the kick. The heavier girl kicks her, pounding her foot into the fragile face and ribs of my Snow Dove. Emily cowers terrified, while Fancy kicks her all over, stomping her without mercy. A male teacher has trouble pulling her off my little girl. I have pressed charges, hoping to God that she will spend a year in jail, though I know that Justice will spin her wheels in the judicial mud, until Fancy Comfort and Emily Sweet are long forgotten. Fancy is a white girl, just like my daughter. There is hardly a power under Heaven that will point an accusatory finger. I know that if Fancy had not been white, she would have been arrested.

Fancy! What are you to me! What am I to thee!

Why should I have compassion that your mother and father are in a cemetery? What is it to me that you are in your older sister's charge, who cares nothing for thee! The beatings you are subject to. The nights you spend alone when she is away at work. Your sister cannot love you, because you are not hers to love. She blames you for her accursed condition. For her lack of total beauty—her inability to attract anything close to her ideal man. What will she do to you tonight, my darling, when she learns that you will be charged with criminal assault? How badly will she beat you with the stick? Rest on the couch, my dear, after the flailing, your young soul bruised—ripe with new bleedings to scar and bare. Yours is the curse of poverty, passed from your dead mother and father. Wherever you go beneath the sun, to what corner of the world, the stench of poverty will follow. And now, the barrier around my Emily is down, because of the Passion. Your suspension will end, and she is left unprotected from thee! Fancy, I pray, have mercy on poor Emily and me!

I am not unaware of the pain you must endure. What agony is it, to relive the loss of your chastity through and through, over and over, by a boyfriend of your sister. A respectable man. Good looking. A man of the church where you and she attend. A man named Tracy Cobb, one Sunday evening. Waiting for Leah Comfort to come home. He coaxes his way into your graces with talk of the Bible and the Lord, does he not? As nice as he is able, in keeping with his personality, he coaxes you into a kiss! His handsome face—his lovely eyes—his smell light a fire in your body, and you let him lay on top of you. He lays on top of you. You tell him no, but his hands do not stop pulling your pants down. But you begin to fight. With all of your 13 year old strength you fight. He holds you down gently, firmly on the couch. The same couch you bleed upon at this moment.

So I won't have to hurt you, he says. He slides your pants all the way off, then your panties. *Its gonna hurt,* you cry. *Its gonna hurt, Tracy.* His is 29 years old, though some think he is younger. He has no feeling. The lust in his body takes his feeling for you away. He quickly takes down his pants. You are afraid to fight now. He lays full on top of you, and you feel your insides splitting up into your stomach. His hands are over your mouth while you scream.

A memory for you, my dear. Two years of this iron burning your mind. From the phantom pain in your bowels, the blue and black fire, his body shaking, the high pitched breathless sound he made in your ear. What did your sister call you when you told her? Did she say my poor little Fancy? Did Leah Comfort pull you to her bosom, for you to wipe your tears away? No. She slapped the blood into your mouth over and over, and called you a *f**king little slut. What f**ckin' lies are you tellin'? He is a church goin' man, Fancy. I cain't even get him to do me half the time!*

Your first woman's beating, my dear. The first beating your sister gave, when you took the curse of being a woman. Fancy! Tend to thine own misery! Don't take her heart from me!

*E*mily is upstairs. Her perfect face has been scratched. Scarred. When eleven o'clock of this same evening rolls around, I wonder where Gerald is. Across infinity, unbounded, I see him. But in the evil present, before the Passion falls, I wonder. I see myself in the mirror of my dresser, being attracted to my own reflection, wishing that I knew why my husband is always late. I am going to ask him after Thanksgiving—when the trees have turned to skeletons, I will inquire of the Shannon Bird, and above what meadow the two of them have flown. After the last Thanksgiving has gone, I will ask my balding prince, what garden whose flowers doth pick, upon what breezes do these petals flow?

I am lucky to be a woman of leisure. I was prized enough by men, so that I was property to be bought. Not some woman to be romanced and loved. But a trophy to be won. I am a possession. I am a kept thing, like an old thoroughbred mare. But at least I am human. I can do a little more than graze. My do-gooding—I keep to the barest minimum. I do not volunteer often. I only give my time at Christmas, and then only to a children's hospital ward, where I volunteer to serve meals. It is in keeping with my avocation, which is food. Cooking, which I do to occupy my time. I gather recipes. I experiment, I burn, I undercook, I perfect. My house is immaculate in between, from high ceiling to carpet. I cook. I clean. I die. It is what I am paid to do.

I desire to be free! I desire to leave this place! Carry me to where the wind roams free above the grassy plain, to carry songs of love from one tree to the next, so far across the prairie! Take me home to the east land, where there is only my daughter for me to tend and love, and we will prepare succulent meals and dine together in our house of isolation, on the rolling sea of green. I pray for the country road to take me home indeed, to the place where I belong! O Lord! Do not burden me with Caitlyn's curse! Father, let this cup pass from me! Do not fetter me in chains, forged by the heat of her twistedness and perversion! Suffer me and my youngest daughter, O Heavenly Father, to escape the face of thy wrath to come!

What my family doesn't know, is the fear that runs through my body. I don't know whose blood in the ancestry has tainted mine, but this fear has plagued me since I was a child. While I spritz this cleanser onto the bathroom tile, I know that deep down, I am terrified of people. Why? I don't really know. It is like being in a room full of strange dogs, all of them quiet. All of them staring.

The 31st of the month enshrouds me while I clean my bathroom. I am alone this Halloween Day. Tonight, every ghost will rise from whatever coffin it is in. I think that my dreams are haunted by them—where I look out the window of my bedroom, and see them drifting in the moonlight. The little ghouls in Target and Walmart plastic roaming the neighborhood begging for candy cannot see what I have seen. The demon spirits that walk the streets, masquerading as spirits of the dead. These drift in and out of their victims with ease, floating in and out of houses, entering through music and television, video games, ouija boards, and the occasional séance or two. Shadows move when candles flicker, where no breeze has shifted or blown. When the Earth has turned past the evening day, and the shadows have grown beyond themselves into night, evil walks the streets of St. Mark's Terrace, and the walkways of Megan Elizabeth Drive.

Tonight, a million miles away, my oldest daughter gives herself away at a party, where they bob for apples in the Blood of the Christ, wearing tight white T-shirts soaked onto their breasts with red wine. Here in Charlotte, I give candy bars to all the greedy ghosts and demons, wondering where it is that my beloved daughter could have gone. With four others—earlier this evening, dressed *posh* in black leather bondage dresses to raise the eyebrows of every one not aware that they are the Spice Girls. My *baby* girl's 15 year old bosom was bursting against the strings crisscrossing the front of them. Her wig was as red as cinnamon. Now, every *scary* touch of the doorbell rattles my nerves to ruin. The homemade *ginger* bread cookie burns my taste buds while I hurry to the door and open it, candy bars in hand, hoping to dazzle with my *sporty* casual look in plain white T-shirt and tight jeans. But no one is there. I close the big white door, amazed by the loudness of sound I hear when I do. A loud, smacking thump against the door. I open it again quickly, in time to see red goo sliding down the door. Egg. Ingeniously needled with red dye through the shell. The yolk is blackish red with blood.

I shall not see my Spice Girls again, until very late. They are going to a party. These last few weeks, since the tiding of Caitlyn Sound, at the coast of Cape Blood, I have looked into my Emily's eyes, to see if she is there. What I see frightens me, though what I worry over as rebellion is likely her socialization. The likely course for a high school freshman—especially one who is as beautiful as she. She does not know the worry I possess—the way I crave her company alone here in the house, away from prying eyes that stare. Emily! My Emily! Where did you go? Into what place? What world? Emily—where have you gone?

And now, the cracking thump again. Though this time I do not open the door, nor do I look to the windows that run with yolks of sunshine, life and hope. My nerves, my poor nerves are on the edge this Halloween night. Is this why I scream, when the rock comes crashing through the window? A large rock, the size of a baseball. As it was in the days of Noah, so shall it be, in the days before the coming of the Son of Man, Daughter of Woman. What child? What home were they raised in? What humanity would hurl a stone in *this* neighborhood, to break one of *these* window panes? Certainly not the Spice Girls. Certainly not my Emily.

Certainly not.

Part Two

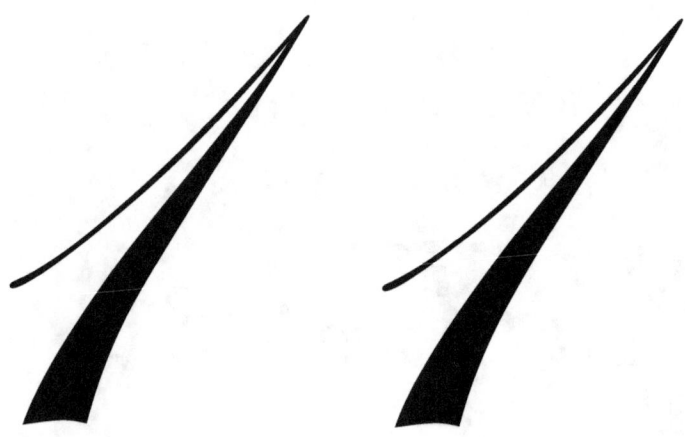

*F*lair will gouge my esteem with colored light.

While I wait for Emily to come home, the evil of the Thriller beckons. Michael Jackson's trial is a benchmark. His very existence is a sign of the times. After the war, a young man whose father is in the military has grown tired of bullying. One day, he calls the three boys over to where he stands. He slams one of the boys in the face with an empty paint can. The boy's face needs stitches. It is a sign of the times. A sixteen year old girl puts her diaphragm in, and has sex with her boyfriend. The diaphragm was a gift from her mother on her sixteenth birthday—it is a sign of the times. They are benchmarks, great and small, along the road to our future.

Long after moonlight has faded, and night has turned to day. Earthquakes, hurricanes, tornadoes, these are signs of the times. The rise of comedy—the fall of tragedy. The loss of love and respect for our fellow man. The rule of Oprah Winfrey, the glory of money and fame. Signs of the times these all are, both one and the same. Spielberg's symphonies of light and sound—orchestras played from the Western Gate. The explosion of Mount St. Helens, the fall of the Berlin Wall of hate—these are signs of the times. The Declaration of Independence. The Chorus of the Slaves, the bloody Civil War itself—the killing of the Man of Lean. When segregation was abolished through the killing of their King—these are signs of the times we are in.

The roaring seas, the ocean waves—the great ships sailing to and fro—the explosion of knowledge in the last 100 years. Our journeys into space. The neverending tide of war and peace, the union of the European nations. As the pirate ship rises from the east—burning blue and black fire, these are signs of the times. The Tri State Tornado of 1925, the 8,000 dead at Galveston Isle. The National Football League—the writer of *The Green Mile*—these are all signs that the end of the age is near. The train of pearls on a string that slammed into the Jovian Sea—the flight of Desperate Housewives from sea to shining sea. Madame Rowling's wizard—the four children of Madame V.C. These are all signs of the coming eschatology.

Jack and Rexella Van Impe. The life and death of Billy Graham. The indescretion of Jimmy Swaggart, and President Clinton, I see. When the arrows are flung from the desert east, and the towers implode poetically.

Theoretically, I see signs of the coming eschatology. Rod Serling and his Twilight Zone--Theodore Geisel and his rhyme. The posthumous life of Emily Dickinson. Longfellow's prose in time. They are from the end of the age. These are signs of the times.

Tonight, when Emily gets home, over an hour late from her curfew, I'm going to fold one of her father's belts in front of her, as if it were going to happen. I fold her father's belt, to see the sign of fear. She tells me she is sorry. She is my daughter again.

My Emily's grave, I tend.

Out here, in the open space of my grassy field, I am a little girl again. My brother and me are at my mother's window, happily ignoring whatever she has to say. A white butterfly captures our attention, to lead us away from the brick house. The day is warm and breezy. The blue sky is hazy with summer's humidity, to keep the cold winds of winter at bay. We run laughing away from the house after the butterfly into the field, which goes the length of two football fields past trees on either side. Far to the other end of this open meadow is a summer cropfield, heavy with the green leaves of its promise. This field stretches to our horizon, to the end of our childhood paradise grown.

I see the mother at the window, calling after the children, who have forgotten the sound of her voice. They listen to the voice of the butterfly, and its calling of their hearts to innocence. I am suddenly away from Paradise, inside where the voice of innocence grows quieter each day. At the palatial house in Charlotte, where I cook and cry, because I remember the look on my daughter's face when I threatened to whip her. The look of terror uncompromised—thoughts of pain and suffering. She was sorrier in her heart than she had ever been. But not because I had threatened to punish her. It was because she had disobeyed her beloved mother, which was against her nature to begin with. And I know that as surely as I roam the Winds of Time, I am guilty for what I have done in my heart, 'til it is cleansed by Him, by the sacrifice He made for me at the Cross.

Why did I take the belt into my hand? What had she done to deserve even the threat? Somewhere, it is written that people never punish righteously. They do it out of sadistic urges. The need to make other people suffer. I think that the transgression was mine. In the deepest part of me, I desire the control over her mind and spirit that I never had with Caitlyn, who raised up early against my feeble attempt to rule her, going beyond my ability to chain her spirit. Somewhere in my body, there is a craving to see my youngest daughter in the bowels of pain. Caused by me, to burn her in blue and black fire, then release her—so that she may praise me for correcting her, and so that she will call me blessed. The craving to whip my daughter burns in me like a seed after a heavy rain, under the rays of the hot suns of May.

What's wrong with you lately, she asks.

What's wrong with you? Those friends you're hanging around with, these grades, and no you are not going to become a cheerleader next year. Ever. Though she asks why, I say only because I said so. That's all the reason you need. I watch the weight of another disappointment crush her little spirit, and a part of me flashes a cold pleasure chill from it. What good am I bringing, restricting her activities? Monitoring every corner of her life? What am I protecting her from? Is it freedom? What evil from along the timeline is she paying for, being made miserable because of me? She is 15 now. And beautiful. They are going to be drawn to her like bees to the brightest flower. Like birds to the tallest tree. How long do I make her pay for the misery and fear that I feel? The resentment I have for my stupid husband and this phony, manufactured life I live?

I hear desperation's call in the water. It screams at me from my daughter's shower. It is the scream of a thousand witches, calling paganism along the line. Their voice, I must obey. While I sit in my bedroom, where I had been waiting for her to take a shower, the water screams, in voices of doom and craving. Causing me to strip my clothes off in lightning time, and put on my bathrobe. In broad hipped splendor, and bosoms heavy from eating, I hurry though the hall with my robe and big white towel. Fate intervenes on my behalf, and the door is not locked. It hardly ever is when she showers—a fear I placed in her early on—what if you fall in the shower while the door is locked? I won't be able to get to you. Even so, I know that the door is unlocked only because her father is out of town. I go in the bathroom and she is at the shower, wrapped up tightly in her towel. In keeping with her sweetness, she does not say appalled, Mom what are you doing? She only looks at me confused, while I toss my decadent towel on the bathroom counter and,lips tucked, untie my deviant robe. Sliding it off in front her. She is speechless at my nudity, my nakedness.

Is your shower broken, she finally says.

No. I just thought I'd join you. Is that OK? I walk over to her and remove her big towel. Her humiliation is my pleasure. Without a word, I take over. Leaning my naked body into the bath to feel the screaming water, the Chorus of the Witches. It is perfect. I get in. In a spirit of *fungalooga* (forced happiness), as though we are in a water park. Her expression arises the depth of confusion, to drift the surface of consternation.

Mom, this is too weird.

No its not. Mothers and daughters take baths together all the time. It's just nobody's business but theirs. It's our special time. Get in. Inside, I take up the shampoo—and tell her to turn around, facing away. I massage the shampoo into her hair until it is lathered. I know how stressful life can be, I say. A strange school. Peer pressure. Curfews. Boys. Best friends. Schoolwork. Teachers. Moms. It's a wonder you can handle it at all. Just relax. After the shampoo is lathered, I take the soap, foaming it greatly in my bare hands. I slide the soap over her shoulders. My nipples against her back is the Chiming of the Bells, which causes me to suppress a powerful shudder. I have to take a quiet, deep breath, to prevent breathing onto her neck.

What churns beneath cultured civility?

The hands of motherhood. Gliding across her daughter's skin. Until every inch of her is foam from top to bottom, until she is a prisoner of the foam. Then I give her the cloth. I'm feeling left out. Don't I get a bath? Her youth and her natural womanhood are captured by the spell of the hidden. The secret that we have begun.

What churns beneath cultured civility?

The daughter's hands, as they rub soap across the mothers neck and shoulders, face to face. Afraid to go lower. In the spirit of fun, I say *hey!*, and give my breasts a thunderous shaking from side to side, which makes her laugh. They're too big, she says. Laughing. She rubs the soapy cloth across my breasts, to hear with her mind the chiming, the music upon the triple D chord, and the melodies they wish in this key.

What churns beneath cultured civility?

I just want you to know how much I love you. And how close I want us to be. And how I don't want anything or anybody in the world to come between us. Cloth and soap aside, I pull her close, pressing myself hard, pushing myself so tightly in the hug. The pleasure is beyond what is known but to an accursed few. Were I not careful, I think that my body would ignite. Inside, there is a scream that lies dormant. A gutteral, animal shriek. It forces me to say, hug me tight. She leans her head to my shoulder, and we stand enraptured by the flow of nerves, the buildup of tensions that cannot be released as they would have it. I let the energy gather in my emotions, to take the alternate course. When they react together, the crying in me expands. Rising, until it is in my eyes and sniffing nose, and running salty down my face.

What's the matter, Mom?

I love you so much that it hurts inside.

Don't cry, Mom…

I love you.

$\mathcal{W}$e make plans unbeknownst to ourselves. Events unfold into circumstances, according to the pattern we have laid. This is our destiny, by the hand of our fate, through the solemn will of God. How many years have I built this house? This new place we live in? Since she was 9 or 10, the long kisses and hugs have been the foundation laid, the compliments and gentle strokes of her bottom have been the walls erected. Our new house is now complete—our enchanted cottage by the sea, by the roaring waves of the high and sounding sea.

What is left that we cannot say? That we cannot feel? This level of control, of domination and submission, the ties that we are binded by, have fettered the two of us together as none would dare hope or imagine, as I now know the full taste of my daughter's kiss, and the feel of her body against mine. What warning does the morning bird sing? What new bereavements do blood and curses bring? What power East of Eden, from the Garden of Antiquity, from the Fall of Woman and Man? What spirit doth reach across the miles, upon the intrepid wind, to gather around my daughter and me—to press us mindlessly together, until we know the kiss? Though it settles my insanity like no drug could ever do, it brings with it a healthy knowledge, a premonition of the crumbling world around us, to soon come crashing upon the house we have built.

Even while they sit at the breakfast table, the two of them, munching cereal, me at the stove for myself, my daughter and me are connected by the unseen. She finishes her cereal, then off to the minions at the door, who have come to steal her away to school. Our bond weakens when proximity is lost, until my body goes cold from her loss, and I know her only in the far reaches of the soul. Gerald speaks something to me about some corporate conocle of copium corpus conclavicus could care less if Carmel cracked and concocted cataclysm. I don't know what he's talking about with that stupid job and I don't care. I do think that it is strange for him to be so cheerful and talkative in the morning. The later he works at night, the more cheerful he is at the breakfast table. He constantly wears a condom on his cockle when he copulates his concubine.

Caitlyn! What have you done to me! My loss of security looms, on the shores of Adultery! He was going to lust her, and then leave her in the

Autumn Day. But his lust has turned to love—in the fall of the Passion Play. Caitlyn! What shall you say tonight! When your father goes away?

Fast food restaurants are a victim of their own popularity. Popularity *does* breed contempt. People stuff their faces with the food from these places and have nothing but criticism for them afterwards. The addicting ingredient in fast food is the taste. I understand this, while I try to swallow parts of this so-called cheeseburger at this upscale do-nothing of an overpriced, overpaid overated place. I enjoy the $15.00 hamburger because I am starved, knowing that Ray Kroc and Dave Thomas are truly under-appreciated in their time. But it is a fine lunch, even if that is more than I can say for my company. The food in these restaurants frustrates me, always being too much money for too little flavor. For dinner some day soon, I am going to lick my manicure from the flavor it has picked up from a fried chicken invented by a man in his 60's, whose recipe for it was rejected 1000 times before it was sold. There is none other on Earth that can compare to it.

Like a greedy, overdeveloped piggy wench I eat my hamburger, wishing I had ordered cheese, while Gerald slops down chicken fettuccini that I know tastes like pure garlic. I can already smell it on his condescending breath.

I'm leaving, he says.

Where are you going? I ask. Disinterested.

The house is yours. You can keep Emily.

Suddenly, the hamburger in my hand is the stupidest, most idiotic thing I have ever seen. I wonder how it is I'll be able to swallow what is in my mouth. Without further chewing, I gulp it down, then take a sip of my distilled water that tastes like tap water. The look on my face is nausea. In my mind, I grab what is left of the $15.00 burger, and fling it, plate first, at his high forehead, cutting his skin to blood. But for posterity, I decide to pretend that my soul has not been frozen into crystal.

What am I going to do about money?

You'll get exactly half of everything. That's over a million dollars cash. You'll be able to take care of you and Emily. The house is in your name. It's worth three quarters of a million dollars.

She must be rich, I say.

My voice hides a tremble. My hands are clasped. My elbows are on the table. My ivory business suit is pristine, though I have no further business to attend.

We can talk about it after it's done, he says. I'll be moving out before Thanksgiving. I'd like for you to tell Emily. I'll tell Caitlyn myself.

May I ask why?

Unable to move, I am. Unable to look up from his fettucini. The green speckles on the noodles add little desirable flavor. In a sempiternal pause, in devastating arrogance, he lets the truth come out.

I don't know, he says.

I want you out tonight.

Look, I said that the house wa—

Tonight, Gerald.

I just wish that Caitlyn would leave school. It is my profound wish, on the eve of the Passion, in days after the Harvest Moon, when Indian summer is gone. What I have known is in the rains of November, where the Autumn falls cold from clouds of mourning. What life I have known is dissolved in the cold, and washed so casually, so unceremoniously away.

The Passion Play

Two weeks before Thanksgiving, on the week of the Passion. Gerald goes in his silver gray convertible, the top sheltering him from the downpour of guilt and trepidation. He rides the current from me to where my daughter sits in her room on her phone, unaware that this is the first sting of poison that will come. She cannot see the wasp formed, gigantic and red, that lies in wait for unsuspecting prey. Unaware, she drifts still, while the giant wasp drifts toward her from parts unknown. From where the life she used to know has been destroyed. Say goodbye, civility! Goodbye, lonely heart! Family life and peace of mind! How many have been killed by this demon she will see today?

Gerald arrives on campus, stinking of his money and cologne, hidden in the unpretentious wear from K mart—a habit pulled from days under poverty and want, at the bottom of the corporate madness climb. He trudges through the cold, even to the music of his breath in fog. He feels premonition, if not déjà vu, for this is a day he has already seen in his heart, and one that he will see again. Adrift. On a current of unknown grieving, under the Forest Moon, Gerald makes his way into the campus ivory tower, to where his daughter is waiting. Already, she knows he is coming, and that he has something important to say. When he arrives at the door, she hugs her father in her tight, young enthusiasm, all smiles, all genuine, all natural for his pleasure.

Her room is her own. Private and cozy. As it has been these last four years, already knowing the feel of financial independence, and the taste of emotional freedom. She has been an adult since even before she left home, though without the pain of life experience. Rich. Happy. Loved. Are these things not desirable for all? Do these three not call to us from the day we leave our mother's womb, to breathe upon our own? The rich girl escorts her father in spirit across the little apartment room to the old bluish sofa, a plush essential, comfortable in its status as used, to not jade her from the comfort of a new one someday soon. She sits with her handsome father, his masculine beauty tainted by loss of hair.

I don't know how to tell you this.

God, did somebody die? Just tell me. It must be important. You could have waited until you came to see the play.

He tells her that yes, he will see the play with her mother and sister. But no longer as their husband and father. Her immediate reaction is to melodrama. Screaming for him about 25 years and to get out, while he holds on to her, covering her mouth with all his strength. Begging for her to please forgive him, even saying once to her, *have mercy*. Caitlyn is touched just enough, so that her melodrama turns lucid, and she sits down again on the sofa—at the other end. She feels exposed in front of her father, legs long and silky smooth in her denim shorts, ala Ms. Catherine Bach. Again, Gerald begs for her to please say something. What do you want me to say, Dad? That after 25 years you're dumping mom so you can hump another woman?

That's not fair. You don't know Shannon.

Is that her name? Shannon?

She gazes a look into his eyes laced with poison, to set his soul afire with guilt, which burns a yellow flame.

Adrift upon the wind, I see Gerald Sweet in the parking lot. In the gray shadow of the ivory tower, holding his eyes open to the autumn cold. His gray coat is a cloak, to disguise his soul of misery, to reflect his goal of prosperity, that which he has achieved a hundred fold and beyond, of which a part of is me. I hear the phone tweeter its call to me, but I have no wish to spill tears into the phone. I leave my oldest daughter to her desperation, even to her scream over the answering machine *pick up the phone, Mom! Mom, pick up!* Now, I am occupied upon the flair of the breeze, kissed by winter's warning. There, I see my husband look upward to the gray skies at me with unseeing eyes, to seek answers from a God that he does not know, while I drift beneath His glory, along the four intrepid winds.

I watch him take his keys to the door of his silver gray—turning them. Inside, he puts the key in the ignition, but he must sit there, and remember the look on his daughter's face when he told her. Unlike when he told me, the hurt of what he has done finally creeps in, and he grips the wheel tighter, and tries not to breathe the sadness wave. But it takes his breath, and Gerald Sweet cries out to the God he has never believed in, and substitutes *Her* name with that of his daughter Caitlyn. Oh, Caitlyn forgive me. Please Caitlyn forgive me. Not even a thought for his youngest Emily, or to the one whose heart he hath pierced with the sword, but only to the other love of his miserable life, who now looks at him with eyes of hate, *greely* eyes—that of Satan at the garden gate.

In mourning for the daughter he once knew, my husband weeps.

I have seen the Ford Taurus Universal in my dreams. It is the most beautiful SUV never made. The best selling vehicle in US history never seen.

This time, I answer the tragic phonecall, knowing what I have to do. I have to confront my daughter on these mistakes that have been made, but knowing why they have come, and what may stop them from returning. I listen to her crying to me on the phone, of her daddy and 25 years, and why aren't I doing everything I can in the world to stop it. Perhaps I am, when I tell her frankly, that I believe that this play is wrong somehow, and I cannot believe the school is letting you stage it. I don't care about the stupid play, she says, what about you and Dad?

Where does the known universe end? It is a question to be answered just as easily. Of this earthbound cosmos, the system of planets we are, I know the realm of their ellipses, the long and short of us, the fast and slow of us, the near and far of us. I know the forces which control our motions, and how it has been compromised by a new, powerful energy. Caitlyn tells me that it has been postponed anyway, until the middle of December, the month of her Virgin Birth, just before Christmas break. Again, I ask—do you think this play is a good idea, Caitlyn? It could offend a lot of people. I hope it does, she snips—bunch of hypocrites. Professor Derrick told me that the hallmark of any good play is controversy. The more, the better. She tells me that the entire cast agreed to take only Thanksgiving Day off, and that they would meet every day after until opening night. She tells me to not bother picking her up this year. I know that she is not coming home for the reason of her parents' impending divorce. Why build a campsite at the base of an active volcano, where the lava may flow on Winter's Eve?

From my home where disaster looms, to the city limits of Greensboro, to the house of Spring Rose. This is not the season, neither the flower, but the name of the light skinned beauty, chosen to don the robes of the Christ, and have herself be crucified. Her mother is Hattie, at her November kitchen, as light skinned and beautiful as her daughter. Though she is called black by those who know, her husband William is as white as snow. William and Hattie's daughter is Spring, as her beauty will attest. Her skin is the palest yellow tint, with big brown eyes of bewitching power; a large, beautiful mouth full of white, smiling teeth, with a laugh that calls everyone to attention. She is the darling of the drama school, chosen in their minds to someday haunt the stages of New York City. She will bare her breasts to be flogged, so that she can shed her blood for the sins of the world.

As the quarter hour chimes my sorrow, I see their daughter Spring, whom the world calls Danielle, preparing a wicked heart to portray the Heart of God. She looks at herself in the mirror, unable to feel sorrow in any form, except when on the stage, shedding tears of an uncommon gift. Danielle Rose is a senior like Caitlyn, on the edge of her freedom. On the eve of the Passion.

I am a troll under a tree. I wait for unsuspecting passers by, then I jump into their faces with a pointed finger, to put out one of their eyes.

Well past the evening day, in shadow and silhouette, I listen to my daughter's oblivion on the phone, while I feel the Mary Jesus embody the Rose of Spring.

I sit in church on the morning after. After the blasphemy of my daughter's will. I am here alone in December. Having no wish to pretend I have a family. What truths are those that the Presbyterian minister sings in baritone, his voice booming over the speaker about the deity of Christ, and the way it is attacked constantly by Satanic forces? By the spirit of

Antichrist—which seems to grow stronger with each passing season. Locally, the University has just committed one of the worst acts of blasphemy I've ever seen, and I thought I had seen everything, he says. He speaks of the lovely Danielle Rose, and how she bore her breasts for the sins of the world. Of how she screamed and writhed naked on the cross until she gave up the ghost to her Heavenly Mother.

I saw it with my own eyes.

In the theatre of my mind, there had played such a great earthquake, such as was not since the beginning of time, which ripped through my soul like a cataclysm. My heart grieves for my family, knowing what course we are set upon, and into what world we must go. It is a long, gray road, on which there is a neverending rain. Along this road, I see into the past, as it is manufactured by some. Of what corruption this is, surely, I do not know. I see Our Lady of the Cross, on the eve of her passion, in the Garden of Gethsemane, on her knees at a great stone. Tears and blood stain the beauty of her face, as she trembles through the impending loss of sanity. Which comes by way of the most blinding headache, with agony in her spirit, even a twinge of fear, both the leading edge of the curse of sin she must bear.

Mother, she whispers, another tear falling to the stone, *let this cup pass from me—not as I will, but as thou will.* She staggers away from the rock—then she falls upon her face, to repeat the prayer to the Holy Mother, even while Andrea Judas Iscariot has begun her walk with the great multitude, and the swords they have taken up against her Lady Messiah. She raises up her head in the moonlight, strengthened by the unseen, until she is able to stand to her feet. She is as tall as most men, and more beautiful, even in suffering, than any other woman ever born. In the strength of the almighty, under the spirit of the Almighty God, she stands in the misty morning dark, looking across the empty garden, ignoring the worried stares from the lady disciple who is the rock, and the disciple of Magdala whom she loves.

After many long, still moments, the torches appear in the night, along with the murmer of voices, and in the garden appears the daughter of perdition, among the commotion of guards and ordinary people, some wielding a glint of light reflecting a sword in their hand. Across the garden, in silence like a wave, they walk to Mary Jesus of Nazareth, waiting to see the witch receive the kiss, that she is the Whore of Galilee. Andrea Judas approaches her Lady and Savior, and kisses her full on the mouth.

$\mathcal{T}$he January chill falls as icy rain, to color our souls to freezing, brushed by a breath of winter cold. After December's mist has conquered warm autumn, there remains a deeper cold, beyond Christmas Day, and into this New Year we are in. Though I am sheltered in this smelly courtroom from the icy rain, my soul still bears the burden of its touch, to shiver my muscles to the bone. These are not bones of the flesh, but of the spirit, which hath beaten and brought me down to nothing.

The judge sits in robed inadequacy. Intelligence lacking— perceptiveness tuned to quacking alone, knowing ducks by no other sign than this. Through spectacles she looks dimly, smartly at a Fancy Comfort, speaking to her about acting like a nice young lady, and *actin' like you got some sense. A pretty young girl like you cain't go around pickin' fights— how unladylike is that?* Her down home, southern ghetto mama wisdom, I can appreciate, though I know she is on the bench by Destiny, rather than ability. The Chosen looks at my daughter with less compassion and understanding, though she is the victim, glancing over us with hardly a care. Wrongly perceiving that Emily is a spoiled, mouthy brat who had it coming. But even I can see that young Fancy exudes a powerful humbleness before proper authority, as a dog fit for killing does when its master appears with a great big stick. This judge has her kitchen momma kettle of caring and misplaced mercy for the fancy doll, and gives her three months of probation for kicking and beating my daughter. When her non-sentence is read, when all is said and done, I glance at the cockle doodle doo haircutted poverty mama judge, and tell her with my eyes of her inferiority to me. In my heart, I am superior. In my soul, my daughter is queen.

Our ride home through the rain is a convocation of circumstances, falling in a sheet of ice. My husband is no longer Emily's father, as her father is no longer my husband. But we are in full fungalooga swing, even laughing at ourselves for no good reason, but perhaps only in relief that we never have to see that courtroom again. Even while phonecalls come down to us in the cold heart of memory, as voices whisper *you gon' die bitch* to my Caitlyn. Even while Fancy is driven home in tears, while her older sister Leah yells at her infinitum, concerning stupidity and ugliness and such, and as to how if you get so much as a detention from this day forward I'm gon beat you like a mangy yard dog *runt* hound, slapping her on the 'runt', causing Fancy's mouth to frown more, as a tear falls where the one before it had gone. Emily and me laugh heartily, in our million dollar contentment, at a dance move she does in smiling, laughing braces, while the icy warnings touch the roof of our gray ride, to talk of Gerald's new, happy life apart from his middle aged wife of 25 years. Would I like to pull a Betty Broderick from my purse, and give it to him and his new fiancé? She is our patron saint. The goddess of abandoned wives, those who are killed inside by their lecherous husbands, who cavalierly laugh afterwards, and dispose of their bloody bodies. My body lies bleeding and broken. In the ice and rain of January's Call. In the epic tiding of Winter.

*T*he voice of retribution calls our name.

When these winter clouds have fallen, a family named DeVine knows from whence all blessings flow, and under whose direction do curses reign. By the light of the silver Mountain Moon, the souls of Cato Devine drive their old blue Cavalier, a 1983 Chevrolet, as old as the bones of my marriage. Backwoods poverty, driving a hobby through the night, to take them to the House of Rose. A vision from God, they believe, come from their father Cato, the backwoods prophet, that Jesse and James were called of God to do this thing that must be. But only by permission of a night dream, the word given to their mother Roberta in her sleep, to inspire the words of the prophet, that Cato and Roberta Devine were called to give their sons charge over vengeance, and the recompence overdue.

James the younger drives to the thick woods, between the highway and paradise. He and Jesse take their chosen path through the suburban woods, to the houses of Heather Trace, and the house on Atwood Drive. Early in the night, when the earth turns past the Evening Day, James and Jesse enter the home of Hattie Rose. Two young, country white men, suddenly in the home of the affluent, to make them wonder why. Without hesitation, the elder sounds the noisest rifle shot through the back of William Rose's head as he runs to the front door, to carry out a failed plan of retreat to a neighbor to call the police. He feels like he has been hit with an aluminum baseball bat, or a two by four block of wood, and then he feels nothing. As to whether he opens his eyes in Hell or Paradise, who is to say? The next rifle shot heard in the neighborhood sends the bullet through Hattie Rose's head, and her brains are splattered red all over her beautiful white refrigerator and cabinets.

When Danielle Spring Rose appears at the bottom of the stairs, she squeaks when the hot barrel touches her neck, and she believes that she can see her father's red brains on the white lampshade and wall. Come on down here, bitch. Look at them big titties, Jesse. Did you call the police? Well, you should have—get your clothes off. Get 'em off, bitch. They have allotted the time, caring nothing for an impending arrest. As they watch the yellow skinned beauty disrobe, James the younger puts down his rifle, leaning it against the wall, while she screams help, help, to the top of her lungs in the January twilight. I see her bra in its D-cupped splendor, white and lacy, being ripped off by James the younger, who is fully aroused in the nude. They are at war with the powers of darkness, with the forces of evil, they care nothing for the police, or whether they will arrive. Jesse stands by, as the Rose of Spring is ripped in two, in the manner of those from the valley of Siddim. I hear the backwoods twang from the younger, deep woods Pentecostal by blood, you gon' learn bitch—I'm gon' teach you to blaspheme. I'm gon' teach you to blaspheme. Her screams are muffled by the cloth gagged into her mouth, and her beautiful face bears tears and no bruise, having not been hit even once in her ordeal. Jesse is obliged by his God to obey the word of the mother, and he disrobes to the music of muffled screams, while the younger holds her immobile on her stomach. Jesse sodomizes the young woman, being done quicker in high pitched animal squealing, feeling more power from it than even his younger brother.

When he is able, he pulls her hair up hard, raising her head up, and James the younger stabs her in the neck, hearing her choke, feeling her soul wrench free. He slices through her neck muscle and bone while Jesse pulls, until they tear her head forthright from her body.

*L*ife and death, this world we spin. Turning time and time again. From where I've gone, to where I've been…the curse of the Passion Play we're in. Dreary days have faded, and my daughters are in my summer again. We are happy, the dead weight of my husband and their father being gone. We stand under the columns, at Megan Elizabeth drive, in the light of the Summer Moon, six months after the play was given. I have accepted this new life as a single woman. Alone, as friend and protector to my princess and my queen. My queen has ended her eighth grade year. She is in the ninth grade tonight, when her sister will be killed.

The elder and the younger DeVine have glided the streets of time itself (since the beheading of the Lady Christ), their white path soaked with her blood. They have not been caught, being intelligent enough to leave no fingerprints through their gloves, and blessed by demonic commission, that no policeman were called that day. The bodies were not found until the following night. What good is DNA evidence then, to identify ghosts in the wind? It is the greatest crime in far away Greensboro's recent memory. It is by them that offences must come, but woe unto them by whom the offence cometh! They have boarded the train to the rest of their dark destiny, arriving here just today, to Charlotte, to do their bidding in the evening. This by only one, James the younger, who already strolls the back yards of our kingdom, at the edge of the atramental woods, looking for my princess to kill. We open the door to our palace, stepping onto the brick entranceway. Wondering, the three of us, how strange it is that a beautiful young man glides across our lawn in the evening day, carrying a double barreled shot gun in his hand...

Hey, witch!

And he pumps the shot gun in slow motion elegance clicking. Is this a prank? I cannot tell, whether it will shoot confetti or a springy snake. I am carried away, to six months ago, when the death threats had begun on my daughter's life, on the night that James DeVine painted the blood red words *thou shalt not suffer a witch to live* on her dorm room door. Like a cancer, it had grown undetected in our lives, until it could be contained no longer, choosing its appointed time of manifestation. This being on our front lawn in June. Under the Summer Moon, when my daughter is killed by a redneck in June. He fires the shot, an explosion of flame, leaping forward in power unrestrained, and I see my daughter's blood blasted in rose pattern through a hole in her back, and the blood assembles in splattering on my face and on the white door behind me...

Her body is thrown back, passing me in slow motion, falling down, slowly downward, until her head strikes the brick beneath our feet. When I look back to the yard, I see nothing, but I feel it running away, to join the elder DeVine, to where their poverty chariot awaits. While I stand there in the cool of Summer's Eve, in a vacuum of sound, my Emily's braces flash the corner of my eye, and screams fall on deaf ears, and I know that my sanity now rests in her hands, even while the rest of Who I am is slowly vanishing away.

In the heart of revelation, I see our Lady on the Cross. The Lady Christ, her naked body bloody from head to foot, her hair glued to her face by blood, crying out *My God! My God! Why hast thou forsaken me?* Another pain of sin lashes her soul from two millennia away, and she trembles in her crown of thorns, with her mouth open, staring wide eyed into the darkened clouds, though not screaming loudly enough to call forth the dead, a miracle done more than once in the years of her ministry. They know, as they look upon the woman, clothed only by a veil of blood, that she is the Messiah. The Christ. Daughter of the Living God.

It is finished. Into thy hands I commend my spirit...

The Lady Christ lowers her head, and she gives up the ghost. When she dies, so do the soldiers' and chief priests' bravery in the great earthquake, which rumbles the holy temple, and splits the temple curtain in two from top to bottom.

I know the cold touch of pain, and the icy touch of misery. They have frozen my soul to ruin. I have retreated from my husband's heart attacked corpse back in Charlotte, and the dead body of my oldest child. I am hidden in eastern North Carolina, too rich for words, considering I have done nothing to earn it by the sweat of my body. But perhaps, there is sweat of the soul and spirit.

These last four years have weighed so heavily upon me, even as I try to escape from the heart of memory. There, I see my daughter Emily and her best friend, whom I once despised, Miss Fancy Comfort. I see the two of them, new graduates, on the back road in the old city, trying to make it across the railroad tracks to a party on time. There is no fireball when the train splatters their bodies to a bloody mess. Emily's luxury car lies upside down from the impact, in a ditch beside the tracks, and her spirit is no longer in her body. Sweet Comfort is ended here, as they were known in the halls of their high school for 3 years, now carried to the Shores of Heaven.

I try not to remember the final nail in my coffin, which happened to me in the spring of Emily's junior year, when she was 17, two years after I saw my ex-husband lowered away. The robbers in our luxury home were both women. The bigger one is hardened. A black woman, brown and beautiful, breasts that dwarf any I have ever seen, and bigger in her body and spirit than I. They take the ten thousand dollars cash from my house in the middle of the day. They beat it out of me, and then the black woman tells her Hispanic friend, take the money and go wait for me. If it's the *last* thing I do, I'm gon' get some. And she returns from the hall to take her part of revenge from me, for a life of poverty and disappointment, holding me down gently, sucking parts of my body while I cry, even biting them to hear me scream. Then she covers my mouth, and removes the attached member she wears from inside her pants. And I feel the blue and black fire split my soul in two.

The demons who are named for Fear of People inhabit my body, as I take my daughter away, in the summer before her final year. Kicking and screaming, I drag her from Hell's Mouth, splitting Sweet Comfort in two.

We arrive here in the heat of summer, under the Prairie Moon, before the rising of the Desert Moon. The Moon which will kill my Emily when she is 18. She drives to Charlotte when she is 18, after high school graduation, after acceptance to Caitlyn's cursed university, after my life has already ended, to take her and Fancy to a party. What am I to fear, since my daughter has already haunted these roads 15 times in the 180 day senior school year to her best friend? What is a mother to do, when the Martin County Sheriff escorts death directly to her door, to tell her, you can never know, never again will you know, where it is that your Beloved daughter could have gone?

I find her body, and bring it here, away from the curse of the Passion Play, to bury her on my property among the trees, beneath the prairie green. But in this body, I have no power. So I rest here on the bed, to put it to sleep with my blue and white pills. And now, I am able to see the passion of my *true* Lord and Savior, and that of the blasphemous Whore of Galilee, and the beheading of the abomination, the Lady Christ. The judgment of my adulterous husband, clutching his chest in his office and dying even before the ambulance arrived. The killing of Caitlyn Sweet, the capture of the brothers Devine, who are turned in by their own mother, so she can sell their story for a fortune. I can see the taking of my chastity, and the dying of Emily Sweet. As a spirit, I drift through all of it, across the timeline forward and back again. As a spirit, I drift undeterred, across the prairie green. Caitlyn's grave lies accursed, and so far from where I've been.

My Emily's grave, I tend.

*E*pilogue

Jonathan Lovejoy

The

Sopperstein Gospel

Jonathan Lovejoy

In the beginning was the Word, the Word was with Mother God, and the Word was Mother God.

The Gospel of Elizabeth
Chapter 1, Verse 1

Jonathan Lovejoy

Addendum

*E*xcerpts from "The Gospel of Elizabeth: The Sopperstein Gospel"
—a theoretical gospel of Jesus Christ as edited from the book of John
(a.k.a. Sarah), King James Version, gender corrected by Ellen Sopperstein,
Ph.D, Women's Studies, Princeton University. Dr. Sopperstein has
proposed the theory that the figure of Jesus Christ was written as a woman
in a lost gospel, and that this manuscript was buried by the early church,
and all copies of this "Gospel of Elizabeth" were destroyed. According to
Dr. Sopperstein, extant references to this lost work place it as the earliest
known gospel, written by Mary's cousin Elizabeth, and that the canonical
gospels were all based upon it, with other material added to them to
establish Christ as a man. In Dr. Sopperstein's book *The Passion Play:
Mary Jesus of Nazareth,* this gospel presents John the Baptist as a female
prophet named Jo Anna, and all of the apostles as women, with Mary Jesus
Christ, a.k.a. Mary Elizabeth as the Messiah, Daughter of the Living God.

Jonathan Lovejoy

Arrested

Chapter 18

1 When Mary Jesus had spoken these words, she went forth with her disciples over the brook Cedron, where was a garden, into the which she entered, and her disciples.

2 And Andrea Judas also, which betrayed her, knew the place: for Mary Jesus ofttimes resorted thither with her disciples.

3 Andrea Judas then, having received a band of men and officers from the chief priests and Pharisees, cometh thither with lanterns and torches and weapons.

4 Mary Jesus therefore, knowing all things that should come upon her, went forth, and said unto them, Whom seek ye?

5 They answered her, Mary Jesus of Nazareth. Mary Jesus saith unto them, I

am she. And Andrea Judas also, which betrayed her, stood with them.

6 As soon then as she had said unto them, I am she, they went backward, and fell to the ground.

7 Then asked she them again, Whom seek ye? And they said, Mary Jesus of Nazareth.

8 Mary Jesus answered, I have told you that I am she: if therefore ye seek me, let these go their way:

9 That the saying might be fulfilled, which she spake, Of them which thou gavest me have I lost none.

10 Then Diana Simone having a sword drew it, and she smote the high priest's servant, and cut off his right ear. The servant's name was Malchus.

11 Then said Mary Jesus unto Simone, Put up thy sword into the sheath: the cup which my Mother hath given me, shall I not drink it?

12 Then the band and the captain and officers of the Jews took Mary Jesus, and bound her,

13 And led her away to Annas first; for he was father in law to Caiaphas, which was the high priest that same year.

14 Now Caiaphas was he, which gave counsel to the Jews, that it was expedient that one woman should die for the people.

15 And Diana Simone followed Mary Jesus, and so did another disciple: that disciple was known unto the high priest, and went in with Mary Jesus into the palace of the high priest.

16 But Simone stood at the door without. Then went out that other disciple, which was known unto the high priest, and spake unto her that kept the door, and brought in Simone.

17 Then saith the damsel that kept the door unto Simone, Art not thou also one of this woman's disciples? She saith, I am not.

18 And the servants and officers stood there, who had made a fire of coals; for it was cold: and they warmed themselves: and Simone stood with them, and warmed herself.

19 The high priest then asked Mary Jesus of her disciples, and of her doctrine.

20 Mary Jesus answered him, I spake openly to the world; I ever taught in the synagogue, and in the temple, whither the Jews always resort; and in secret have I said nothing.

21 Why askest thou me? ask them which heard me, what I have said unto them: behold, they know what I said.

22 And when she had thus spoken, one of the officers which stood by struck Mary Jesus with the palm of his hand, saying, Answerest thou the high priest so?

23 Mary Jesus answered him, If I have spoken evil, bear witness of the evil: but if well, why smitest thou me?

24 Now Annas had sent her bound unto Caiaphas the high priest.

25 And Simone stood and warmed herself. They said therefore unto her, Art not thou also one of her disciples? She denied it, and said, I am not.

26 One of the servants of the high priest, being his kinsman whose ear Simone cut off, saith, Did not I see thee in the garden with him?

27 Simone then denied again: and immediately the cock crew.

28 Then led they Mary Jesus from Caiaphas unto the hall of judgment: and it was early; and they themselves went not into the judgment hall, lest they should be defiled; but that they might eat the passover.

29 Pilate then went out unto them, and said, What accusation bring ye against this woman?

30 They answered and said unto him, If she were not a malefactor, we would not have delivered her up unto thee.

31 Then said Pilate unto them, Take ye her, and judge her according to your law. The Jews therefore said unto her, It is not lawful for us to put any woman to death:

32 That the saying of Mary Jesus might be fulfilled, which she spake, signifying what death she should die.

33 Then Pilate entered into the judgment hall again, and called Mary Jesus, and said unto her, Art thou the Queen of the Jews?

34 Mary Jesus answered him, Sayest thou this thing of thyself, or did others tell it thee of me?

35 Pilate answered, Am I a Jew? Thine own nation and the chief priests have delivered thee unto me: what hast thou done?

36 Mary Jesus answered, My kingdom is not of this world: if my kingdom were of this world, then would my servants fight, that I should not be delivered to the Jews: but now is my kingdom not from hence.

37 Pilate therefore said unto her, Art thou a queen then? Mary Jesus answered, Thou sayest that I am a queen. To this end was I born, and for this cause came I into the world, that I should bear witness unto the truth. Every one that is of the truth heareth my voice.

38 Pilate saith unto her, What is truth? And when he had said this, he went out again unto the Jews, and saith unto them, I find in her no fault at all.

39 But ye have a custom, that I should release unto you one at the passover: will ye therefore that I release unto you the Queen of the Jews?

40 Then cried they all again, saying, Not this woman, but Barabbas. Now Barabbas was a robber.

Jonathan Lovejoy

Crucified

Chapter 19

1 Then Pilate therefore took Mary Jesus, and scourged her.

2 And the soldiers platted a crown of thorns, and put it on her head, and they put on her a purple robe,

3 And said, Hail, Queen of the Jews! and they smote her with their hands.

4 Pilate therefore went forth again, and saith unto them, Behold, I bring her forth to you, that ye may know that I find no fault in her.

5 Then came Mary Jesus forth, wearing the crown of thorns, and the purple robe. And Pilate saith unto them, Behold the woman!

6 When the chief priests therefore and officers saw her, they cried out, saying, Crucify her, crucify her. Pilate saith unto them, Take ye her, and crucify her: for I find no fault in her.

7 The Jews answered her, We have a law, and by our law she ought to die, because she made God as a woman, and herself the Daughter of God.

8 When Pilate therefore heard that saying, he was the more afraid;

9 And went again into the judgment hall, and saith unto Mary Jesus, Whence art thou? But Mary Jesus gave him no answer.

10 Then saith Pilate unto her, Speakest thou not unto me? knowest thou not that I have power to crucify thee, and have power to release thee?

11 Mary Jesus answered, Thou couldest have no power at all against me, except it were given thee from above: therefore he that delivered me unto thee hath the greater sin.

12 And from thenceforth Pilate sought to release her: but the Jews cried out, saying, If thou let this woman go, thou art not Caesar's friend: whosoever maketh herself a queen speaketh against Caesar.

13 When Pilate therefore heard that saying, he brought Mary Jesus forth, and sat down in the judgment seat in a place

that is called the Pavement, but in the Hebrew, Gabbatha.

14 And it was the preparation of the passover, and about the sixth hour: and he saith unto the Jews, Behold your Queen!

15 But they cried out, Away with her, away with her, crucify her. Pilate saith unto them, Shall I crucify your Queen? The chief priests answered, We have no queen. We have no king but Caesar.

16 Then delivered he her therefore unto them to be crucified. And they took Mary Jesus, and led her away.

17 And she bearing her cross went forth into a place called the place of a skull, which is called in the Hebrew Golgotha:

18 Where they crucified her, and two other with her, on either side one, and Mary Jesus in the midst.

19 And Pilate wrote a title, and put it on the cross. And the writing was MARY JESUS OF NAZARETH THE QUEEN OF THE JEWS.

20 This title then read many of the Jews: for the place where Mary Jesus was crucified was nigh to the city: and it was written in Hebrew, and Greek, and Latin.

21 Then said the chief priests of the Jews to Pilate, Write not, The Queen of the

Jews; but that she said, I am Queen of the Jews.

22 Pilate answered, What I have written I have written.

23 Then the soldiers, when they had crucified Mary Jesus, took her garments, and made four parts, to every soldier a part; and also her coat: now the coat was without seam, woven from the top throughout.

24 They said therefore among themselves, Let us not rend it, but cast lots for it, whose it shall be: that the scripture might be fulfilled, which saith, They parted my raiment among them, and for my vesture they did cast lots. These things therefore the soldiers did.

25 Now there stood by the cross of Mary Jesus her mother, and her mother's sister, and Mary Magdalene.

26 When Mary Jesus therefore saw her mother, and the disciple standing by, whom she loved, she saith unto her mother, Woman, behold thy daughter!

27 Then saith she to the disciple, Behold thy mother! And from that hour that disciple took her unto her own home.

28 After this, Mary Jesus knowing that all things were now accomplished, that the scripture might be fulfilled, saith, I thirst.

29 Now there was set a vessel full of vinegar: and they filled a spunge with vinegar, and put it upon hyssop, and put it to her mouth.

30 When Mary Jesus therefore had received the vinegar, she said, It is finished: and she bowed her head, and gave up the ghost.

31 The Jews therefore, because it was the preparation, that the bodies should not remain upon the cross on the sabbath day, (for that sabbath day was an high day,) besought Pilate that their legs might be broken, and that they might be taken away.

32 Then came the soldiers, and brake the legs of the first, and of the other which was crucified with her.

33 But when they came to Mary Jesus, and saw that she was dead already, they brake not her legs:

34 But one of the soldiers with a spear pierced her side, and forthwith came there out blood and water.

35 And she that saw it bare record, and her record is true: and she knoweth that she saith true, that ye might believe.

36 For these things were done, that the scripture should be fulfilled, A bone of her shall not be broken.

37 And again another scripture saith, They shall look on her whom they pierced.

38 And after this Joseph of Arimathaea, being a disciple of Mary Jesus, but secretly for fear of the Jews, besought Pilate that he might take away the body of Mary Jesus: and Pilate gave him leave. He came therefore, and took the body of Mary Jesus.

39 And there came also Nicodemus, which at the first came to Mary Jesus by night, and brought a mixture of myrrh and aloes, about an hundred pound weight.

40 Then took they the body of Mary Jesus, and wound it in linen clothes with the spices, as the manner of the Jews is to bury.

41 Now in the place where she was crucified there was a garden; and in the garden a new sepulchre, wherein was never man yet laid.

42 There laid they Mary Jesus therefore because of the Jews' preparation day; for the sepulchre was nigh at hand.

Jonathan Lovejoy

Resurrected

Chapter 20

1 The first day of the week cometh Mary Magdalene early, when it was yet dark, unto the sepulchre, and seeth the stone taken away from the sepulchre.

2 Then she runneth, and cometh to Diana Simone, and to the other disciple, whom Mary Jesus loved, and saith unto them, They have taken away the HOLY MOTHER out of the sepulchre, and we know not where they have laid her.

3 Simone therefore went forth, and that other disciple, and came to the sepulchre.

4 So they ran both together: and the other disciple did outrun Simone, and came first to the sepulchre.

5 And she stooping down, and looking in, saw the linen clothes lying; yet went she not in.

6 Then cometh Diana Simone following her, and went into the sepulchre, and seeth the linen clothes lie,

7 And the napkin, that was about her head, not lying with the linen clothes, but wrapped together in a place by itself.

8 Then went in also that other disciple, which came first to the sepulchre, and she saw, and believed.

9 For as yet they knew not the scripture, that she must rise again from the dead.

10 Then the disciples went away again unto their own home.

11 But Mary stood without at the sepulchre weeping: and as she wept, she stooped down, and looked into the sepulchre,

12 And seeth two angels in white sitting, the one at the head, and the other at the feet, where the body of Mary Jesus had lain.

13 And they say unto her, Woman, why weepest thou? She saith unto them, Because they have taken away my HOLY MOTHER, and I know not where they have laid her.

14 And when she had thus said, she turned herself back, and saw Mary Jesus standing, and knew not that it was Mary Jesus.

15 Mary Jesus saith unto her, Woman, why weepest thou? whom seekest thou? She, supposing her to be the gardener woman, saith unto her, Madame, if thou have borne her hence, tell me where thou hast laid her, and I will take her away.

16 Mary Jesus saith unto her, Mary. She turned herself, and saith unto her, Mother.

17 Mary Jesus saith unto her, Touch me not; for I am not yet ascended to my Mother: but go to my brethren, and say unto them, I ascend unto my Mother, and your Mother; and to my God, and your God.

18 Mary Magdalene came and told the disciples that she had seen the HOLY MOTHER, and that she had spoken these things unto her.

19 Then the same day at evening, being the first day of the week, when the doors were shut where the disciples were assembled for fear of the Jews, came Mary Jesus and stood in the midst, and saith unto them, Peace be unto you.

20 And when she had so said, she shewed unto them her hands and her side.

Then were the disciples glad, when they saw the HOLY MOTHER.

21 Then said Mary Jesus to them again, Peace be unto you: as my Mother hath sent me, even so send I you.

22 And when she had said this, she breathed on them, and saith unto them, Receive ye the Holy Ghost:

23 Whose soever sins ye remit, they are remitted unto them; and whose soever sins ye retain, they are retained.

24 But Eva, one of the twelve, called Lydia, was not with them when Mary Jesus came.

25 The other disciples therefore said unto her, We have seen the HOLY MOTHER. But she said unto them, Except I shall see in her hands the print of the nails, and put my finger into the print of the nails, and thrust my hand into her side, I will not believe.

26 And after eight days again her disciples were within, and Eva with them: then came Mary Jesus, the doors being shut, and stood in the midst, and said, Peace be unto you.

27 Then saith she to Eva, Reach hither thy finger, and behold my hands; and reach hither thy hand, and thrust it into my side: and be not faithless, but believing.

28 And Eva answered and said unto her, My HOLY MOTHER and my God.

29 Mary Jesus saith unto her, Eva, because thou hast seen me, thou hast believed: blessed are they that have not seen, and yet have believed.

30 And many other signs truly did Mary Jesus in the presence of her disciples, which are not written in this book:

31 But these are written, that ye might believe that Mary Jesus is Christ Elizabeth, the Daughter of God; and that believing ye might have life through her name.

ABOUT THE AUTHOR

Jonathan Lovejoy is a graduate of the University of North Carolina at Greensboro, with a B.A. in Religious Studies, and a graduate of Liberty University with an M.A. in Theological Studies. He currently lives in Winston Salem, North Carolina.

For more info on the author's life and career, visit jonathanlovejoy.com

www.ingramcontent.com/pod-product-compliance
Lightning Source LLC
Chambersburg PA
CBHW060644130626
46555CB00002B/956